A· PRESENT· FOR·
A·GOOD·CHILD·

THREE

LITTLE PIGS

Allen D. Bragdon Publishers, Inc.

Bedtime Classics Library

Children's classics
in heirloom facsimile editions

Copyright by Allen D. Bragdon Publishers, Inc.

All rights reserved under Pan American
and International Copyright Conventions.
No part of this book may be reproduced in any form
without permission in writing from the publisher.

Published by Allen D. Bragdon Publishers, Inc.
Tupelo Road, South Yarmouth, MA 02664

Distributed to the book trade in the U.S. and Canada
by The Talman Company, New York

Manufactured in Hong Kong 3 4 5 6 7 8 9 10

Library of Congress Cataloging in Publication Data

The Three Little Pigs

(Bedtime Classics Library; 2)
[1. Folklore—Scotland. 2. Pigs—Folklore]
I. Series
PZ8.1.T383   1987b   398.2'4529734   (E)   86-33407
ISBN 0-916410-38-2

Three Little Pigs

ONCE upon a time, when pigs could talk and no one had ever heard of bacon, there lived an old piggy mother with her three little sons, Spotty, Curly-tail and Little Runt.

They had a very pleasant home in the middle of an oak forest, and were all just as happy as the day was long, until one sad year the acorn crop failed; then, indeed, poor Mrs. Piggy-wiggy often had hard work to make both ends meet.

One day she called her sons to her, and, with tears in her eyes, told them that she must send them out into the wide world to seek their fortune.

At first they almost cried, but then they thought it would be fun to build their own homes, and their mother told them, she was sure they would all be very good little pigs.

THREE LITTLE PIGS

She kissed them all round, and the three little pigs set out upon their travels, each taking a different road, and carrying a bundle slung on a stick across his shoulder.

Spotty walked toward the South, Curly-tail walked toward the North, but little Runt walked toward the rising sun, and all the time he was thinking what a fine little house he would build.

THREE LITTLE PIGS

Curly-tail, the first little pig, had not gone far before he met a man carrying a bundle of straw; so he said to him: "Please, man, give me that straw to build me a house?" The man was very good-natured, so he gave him the bundle of straw, and the little pig built a pretty little house with it.

The house was very pretty to look at, but being built of nothing but straw, the wind could blow it away, but Curly-tail never thought of that.

No sooner was it finished, and the little pig thinking of going to bed, than a wolf came along, knocked at the door, and said: "Little pig, little pig, let me come in."

But the Curly-tail laughed softly, and answered: "No, no, by the hair of my chinny-chin-chin."

The said the wolf sternly: "I will *make* you let me in; for I'll huff, and I'll puff, and I'll blow your house in!"

So he huffed and he puffed and he blew the straw house in. Then he quickly gobbled up the little pig in three bites.

Spotty, the second little pig also met a man, and *he* was carrying a bundle of furze; so Spotty said, politely: "Please, kind man, will you give me that furze to build me a house?"

The man agreed, and Spotty set to work to build himself a snug little house before the night came on.

But furze is light shrubby stuff, that belongs to the bean family, and never was meant to be used for house-building; however, Spotty never thought of that and was much pleased with his little house.

It was scarcely finished when the wolf came along, and said. "Little pig, little pig, let me come in." "No, no, by the hair of my chinny-chin-chin," answered Spotty. "Then I'll huff, and I'll puff, and I'll blow your house in!" said the wolf.

So he huffed and he puffed, and he puffed and he huffed, and at last he blew the house in, and gobbled the little pig up in a trice.

Now, the third pig, Little Runt, met a man with a load of bricks and mortar, and he said, "Please, man, will you give me those bricks to build a house with?"

So the man gave him the bricks and mortar and a little trowel as well, and the little pig built himself a nice strong little house. As soon as it was finished the wolf came to call, just as he had done to the other little pigs, and said. "Little pig, little pig, let me in!" But the little pig answered: "No, no, by the hair of my chinny-chin-chin."

"Then," said the wolf "I'll huff, and I'll puff, and I'll blow your house in." Well, he huffed and he puffed, and he puffed and he huffed, and he huffed and he puffed; first he huffed on the north side, and then he puffed on the south side, and then he ran around to the east side, and finished up on the west side, but he could *not* get the house down.

At last he had no breath left to huff and puff with, so he sat down outside the little pig's house and thought for awhile. Presently he called out: "Little pig, I know where there is a nice field of turnips." "Where?" said the little pig. "Behind the farmer's house, three fields away, and if you will be ready to-morrow morning I will call for you, and we will go together and get some breakfast."

"Very well," said the little pig; "I will be sure to be ready. What time do you mean to start?" "At six o'clock," replied the wolf.

Well, the wise little pig got up at five, scampered away to the field, and brought home a fine load of turnips before the wolf came. At six o'clock the wolf came to the little pig's house and said: "Little pig, are you ready?"

"Ready!" cried the little pig. "Why, I have been to the field and come back again long ago, and now I am busy boiling a potful of turnips for breakfast."

The wolf was very angry indeed; but he made
up his mind to catch the little pig somehow or
other; so he told him that he knew where there
was a nice apple-tree. "Where?" said the little
pig. "Round the hill in the squire's orchard,"
the wolf said. "So if you will promise to play me
no tricks, I will come for you to-morrow morning
at five o'clock, and we will go there together and
get some rosy-cheeked apples."

The next morning piggy got up at four o'clock and was off and away long before the wolf came. But the orchard was a long way off, and besides, he had the tree to climb, which is a difficult matter for a little pig, so that before the sack he had brought with him was quite filled he saw the wolf coming towards him.

He was dreadfully frightened, but he thought it better to put a good face on the matter, so when the wolf said: "Little pig, why are you here before me? Are they nice apples?" he replied at once: "Yes, very; I will throw down one for you to taste. Will you have a red one or a yellow one? A sweet apple or sour one? There are all kinds on this tree; I'll find a good one."

So he picked an apple and threw it so far that whilst the wolf was running to fetch it Little Runt had time to jump down and scamper away home. And when he got into his little house again, he shut the door tight, and locked it, and went to bed, pulling the covers up tight around him.

The next day the wolf came again, and told the little pig that there was going to be a fair in the town that afternoon, and asked him if he would go with him.

"Oh! yes," said the pig, "I will go with pleasure. What time will you be ready to start?"

"At half-past three," said the wolf.

Of course, the little pig started long before the time, went to the fair, and bought a fine large butter-churn, and was trotting away with it on his back when he saw the wolf coming.

"My Goodness," said Little Runt. "I'm afraid he will get me this time! If I hadn't stopped to ride in the merry-go-round I would have been safe at home."

He did not know what to do, so he crept into the churn to hide, and, by so doing, started it rolling.

Down the hill it went, rolling over and over, with the little pig squeaking inside.

The wolf could not think what the strange thing rolling down the hill could be; so he turned tail and ran away home in a fright without ever going to the fair at all. He went to the little pig's house to tell him how frightened he had been by a large round thing which came rolling past him down the hill.

"Ha! ha!" laughed the little pig, "so I frightened you, eh? I had been to the fair and I saw everything. I rode in the merry-go-round, and I bought taffy, and a balloon, and some new collar-buttons, and last of all, I bought a butter-churn; when I saw you I got inside it and rolled down the hill."

This made the wolf so angry that he declared that he *would* eat up the little pig, and that nothing should save him, for he would jump down the chimney.

"You cannot get up to the chimney," said Little Runt.

"Yes I can," said the wolf. "I will climb up the vines, run along the roof and jump right down the chimney."

But the clever little pig hung a pot full of water over the hearth and then made a blazing fire, and just as the wolf was coming down the chimney he took off the cover and in fell the wolf. In a second the little pig had popped the lid on again.

Then he boiled the wolf, and ate him for supper, and after that he lived quietly and comfortably all his days, and was never troubled again!

BEDTIME CLASSICS LIBRARY
Museum-quality reproductions of classic old editions in full color

Each of these volumes is at once a precious object of folk art, a classic storybook for a child to read or be read from, and a perfect gift for a child who will remember it always and pass it on as a family heirloom.

This is a genuine piece of Americana that must be enjoyed by a new generation of children. The Bedtime Classics Library is to be commended for its efforts in presenting treasured classics from the past to children of today.
—C. Clodfelter, Ph.D., Chairman, Department of Education, The University of Dallas

Little Red Riding Hood

The text is a retold version of the French *Le Petit Chaperon Rouge* collected by Charles Perrault in 1696 and originally published in his work entitled *The Tales of Mother Goose*. This retelling eliminates the violent details in the original French tale, so it is suitable for young children.

This heirloom facsimile is cloth-bound, sewn with sturdy thread, and has those lovely, old-fashioned drawings at every turn. The colors upon yellowed pages give this the warmth of an actual antique.
—Kristiana Gregory, *Los Angeles Times*

ISBN 0-916410-35-8